Stroll Down the Crooked Path

Take a stroll with me, if you will, down this crooked path of life.

Introduction

Welcome to my twisted mind. If you are here of your own volition, then I applaud you. If you got lost on the path, then I suggest you turn back now. The twists and turns ahead are not for the weak willed. Dig deep, brave traveler and abide the rules.

Watch the shadows.

Do not whistle after dark.

Eyes forward.

He cannot harm you if you ignore him.

Keep your appendages on the path.

Do not take any food offered.

And lastly, you are never alone.

Table of contents

- Choices
- A Feeling
- Coincidence or Causality
- Bad Dreams
- Tap
- The Problem With Tony
- When the Cicadas Dance
- A Simple Task
- A Trip to Lock Head Woods

Choices

"Right, left, or middle?"
Two gleaming rows of pointed teeth shone through the darkness, barely moving as the words slipped through the veil of my unconsciousness. I shook my head, trying to make myself more aware of just what that disembodied voice was asking of me.

"Again, Mr. Mills right, left, or middle? Choose quickly time is a factor."

"Right, left, or middle what? I don't understand what you are asking me!"

Two milky white orbs appeared above the teeth; their gaze burned into me even with no discernible pupils.

"Quite simple really."

Their gaze shifted towards a trio of doors with no markings, each one the same as the last.

"You now have three minutes to make a decision Mr. Mills right, left, or middle."

"What's behind the doors? Why are you doing this? Please, just tell me!"

"Two minutes forty-seven seconds left, Mr. Mills."

The thing's teeth and eyes never changed or showed a glimmer of emotion. I could feel an oppressive emptiness all around me. No light shone anywhere in this abyss, aside from my captor's face. I wanted to run, but those teeth kept me rooted in place.

"One minute, Mr. Mills. I suggest you choose now."

"And what if I don't? Then what?"

With no perceivable movement, I could tell he was smiling, a flame glistening in his milky white eyes. His teeth separated, showing off every needle-thin point.

"I grow tired of waiting Mr. Mills and waiting well waiting makes…. me…. famished."

"LEFT I choose LEFT!"

"Good choice Mr. Mills. Now please proceed to the left-hand door."

As if on cue, my legs uprooted themselves and started for the left-hand door. Pure dread crept throughout my body. I wanted to run, shout, scream, and bite any bit of defiance I could muster, but I couldn't. Those teeth crushed any fight left in my body. We arrived at the door and my captor pushed it open.

"It's been a pleasure, Mr. Mills."

I stopped in the middle of the room as the door slammed shut behind me. Pure white walls glared back at me; no light hung from the ceiling, yet the walls were bright enough to make me squint.

"I don't understand what you want…"

The words were torn from my lips and replaced by a guttural scream as barbed spikes shot through my feet. I tried moving them and let loose another howl as the barbs tore through the surrounding flesh.

"Simple, Mr. Mills. I wanted you to choose and choose you did. Now from this room, based on your size and weight, it will take roughly 30 minutes to bleed out, provided you don't struggle and remain calm."

My pulse quickened, and my stomach turned sour. I spewed bile across the ground. I tried to kneel, but the barbs kept me upright.

"WHY just answer me already," I screamed, spitting bile and phlegm at what was once the disembodied teeth and eyes. His form had changed into a humanoid wisp of black smoke.

"Your choice this time allows me a little more time to explain without getting off schedule, so I will humor you, Mr. Mills."

The milky white eyes surveyed the pooling blood, hungrily my captor let out a soft purr from deep within his Smokey form.

"You see, Mr. Mills, when you were alive you made some very, very bad choices, sins if you so choose to call them."

His eyes were glued to my feet, the wispy form slowly solidifying as more of my blood poured from the holes in my flesh.

"You made choices "sins" in your life with no hesitation that hurt people, some major, some minor, so now you get to spend eternity with me."

His teeth spread in a hungry grin, eyes dancing from my feet to the blood now trickling toward him.

"Eternity with me choosing a different door and a different punishment each time resetting the clock only when you finally perish."

My head was getting light, the feeling in my legs fading as the blood left them.

"What... what do you mean reset?"

"Simple, Mr. Mills, after we finish in whichever room strikes your fancy. You are restored wholly with your memory reset back in the main chamber. Where we begin the choice again."

"What kind of sick place is this?"

"I believe your religion refers to this as hell, Mr. Mills."
Black spots were forming at the edges of my vision now, his form now solid swam in and out of focus.

"I was hoping you would struggle a bit more, to be honest. This is one of the longer punishments, and as I've said before, waiting makes me so very, very hungry."

His teeth stretched into an enormous smile.

"This is now your 375th choice. I've come to discover the blood picks up a sweet taste if the punishment takes longer and I have several sweet teeth to satisfy Mr. Mills."

I spat in his direction, my phlegm landing pitifully several inches in front of him. My last act of defiance caused a joyous laugh to burst forth from my captor's mouth. The world faded out, and I saw in my last seconds those teeth rushed toward my falling body.

"Right, left, or middle?"

Two gleaming rows of teeth shone through the darkness, barely moving as the words slipped through the veil of my unconsciousness.

A feeling

It's been gnawing at me all day that I've forgotten something. I go through the mental checklist; door locked, oven off, windows closed, and …. And what? I shake it off for a while and then something pricks at me again. It had to be something important, but if it was so important, I should be able to remember it.

I went through the motions at work, handed in the papers where needed, and nodded at all the right places during a conversation. All the while going over my list; Door check, oven check, window check, and …… damn it, what was it? My boss caught on to my plight halfway through the day and let me leave since I was ahead of schedule.

Boarding the train and checking my list; door, oven, window, and…… I bumped into a rough-looking man with a grunt. I quickly took my seat and lost myself in my memory, trying to find what it was that was eluding me. The train hissed to a stop, and I was nowhere closer to remembering what it was that I did or didn't remember to do. I trudged my way up to my apartment building and retraced my steps.

Door locked, of course, the windows all locked, the oven not even slightly warm. I walked every inch of my apartment, trying my hardest to remember what I had forgotten. There were no calendar reminders, no sticky notes on the fridge, just what had I forgotten. I turned the TV on, knowing there was no way I could even remotely pay attention to it. My mind was too focused on remembering.

I managed to doze off for a short time while the news anchor droned on. I stretched and made some food, the gnawing at the back of my mind momentarily made mute by my roaring stomach. Opening the fridge and making a slop of a meal from day-old leftovers, I pondered again just what was I forgetting.

A knock startled me, causing me to drop the plate I was holding. The peephole gave a clear view of two uniformed officers. Before they could announce themselves, it hit me, finally, in a moment of glorious and horrendous clarity.

"Police open up!"

No, I don't think I will. My mind was finally clear for the first time today. I blew out the oven pilot light and turned on the gas. I remembered it all so clearly. Everything had been perfect until she screamed. She screamed and fought for her life. After I killed her, a neighbor had come running from the neighboring apartment. I panicked and ran down the wrong alley. There was a surveillance camera at the mouth of that alleyway.

No use crying over spilled milk. I had a nice run time to go out with a bang. As I struck my match, I heard,

"Shit, we got the wrong building. It's the one a block over."

"Coincidence or causality?"

"What are you talking about, Nick?"

"What do you think this horror flick is based on?" Nick said.

"I'm not following you," replied Sam.

"It's simple. All horror movies now are based on coincidence or causality. It's a coincidence that the couple moves into the house with the possessed doll. It's causality that the teens get murdered messing with the Ouija board. No matter what movie it is, it's always based on those two. If someone made a movie without using either of them, people might get scared, you know," Nick explained.

"I.... I guess you could say it's umm," said Sam.

"Any day now, Sam, it's a simple question of coincidence or causality. I've shown you the first few minutes you should be able to guess by now." Said, Nick

"Look man, I don't know what you're trying to get at alright!" Yelled Sam

"Sam, Sam, Sam…… do you think I'm stupid? I've explained it clearly, I would think. Was the clip I showed you of my useless cheating girlfriend getting her skin flayed open coincidence or causality?"

"Causality I guess, man! Jesus, just let me go. You were going to break up with her, anyway." Sam howled.

"Causality exactly! Hallelujah, he does have more than one brain cell left!"

"Look, I'm sorry man, just let me go and we can forget this whole thing ever happened I won't tell…. Nick, what…. what are you doing?"

"Let me ask another question, Sam. Do you think it's a coincidence you're tied up in my bed? The same bed you and her defiled in my absence!"

"I…"

"Don't bother answering. It's all rhetorical at this point. No matter how much coincidence there is, causality is always at the real heart of the matter Sam. The cause and effect of what you did will be simple. I left enough DNA of yours with her, along with a
typed-out letter from your computer admitting guilt."

"You sick fu…"

"Now, now, no need for your last words to be so negative. Now for your causality. I've given you a nice little tranquilizer. It will appear self-administered. I worked hard on it, but it won't matter. The lit oven and broken gas line you rigged will deal with the rest." Nick started for the door.

"Nick…… please…"

"Bye Sam, if by some coincidence you make it out well, I'll be waiting for my causality."

Bad dreams

"How long have you been having this issue, Michael?"

I stared at Dr. Mills across the coffee table and brooded.

"My whole life, I guess, I don't know." I shrugged my shoulders and stared at the table.

"Not dreaming is no cause for concern, Michael. It can be simple things like not getting enough REM sleep or bigger things like sleep apnea." Dr. Mills scribbled on his pad for a minute, and I let the silence rule for a little longer.

"I've had a full physical and a sleep study doctor," I told him, just a suggestion of aggravation in my voice.

"Oh, and what did the doctor tell you?" Dr. Mills scribbled more on his little notepad; I don't know why, but that sound made me want to snap his pen.

"They told me I'm healthy, no sleep apnea, and I entered REM sleep as I should." I felt stupid sitting here talking about this. I didn't even want to do this.

"So, a completely healthy 30-year-old male with no sleep issues, no prior traumatic events, and no recent head injuries, correct?" Dr. Mills stared down his rimless glasses at me.

"Yeah," I answered dejectedly.

"Why are you here, Michael?"

"I wake up drenched in sweat and…"

"And what, Michael?" Dr. Mills is leaning forward now, pen and paper forgotten on his side table.

"And I scream so loud I've had the cops called more than once! I've had to move three times in the last year because of noise complaints. I've paid more than enough for medical bills for damage to my throat. I just want to know why, doctor!"

Dr. Mills reclined in his seat and stared at me until I got myself back under control. He picked his notebook back up and I could see him writing "psychotic" and "danger to society" repeatedly. He had no right to judge me. I just wanted to know what was wrong with me and what scared me so much in my sleep.

"Michael, this is a safe place. You can express your frustrations and anxieties here openly as long as you keep it to a safe level."

"Okay, I can do that." Dr. Mills smiled at me and put his notebook away again. He sat forward, steepled his fingers, and breathed deeply.

"We don't have much time left, Michael, so I want to pinpoint exactly what it is that you want to accomplish here."

"I want to be normal again, doctor. How hard is that to understand?" I clenched my fist and stared into his eyes. He returned my gaze and kept on smiling.

"I want you to hypnotize me, I want you to ask about repressed memories, I want you to help me fix this!" I slapped the side of my head for emphasis. Dr. Mills got up and paced around the room touching some of his Knick knacks and came to a stop behind me. He placed a hand on both of my shoulders and took a deep breath, exhaling slowly.

"Michael, if I fixed you, I'd starve." He patted my shoulders and walked back towards the window.

"I'm sure you will find other clients. My measly $100 isn't going to bankrupt you." I laughed nervously at his demeanor and fidgeted in my seat.

"Money means nothing to me, Michael. What do you remember?" Dr. Mills asked calmly.

"I told you earlier I don't remember any of the dreams." Dr. Mills cut me off abruptly.

"About today Michael, what do you remember from today specifically?" He finally turned around and gazed at me. I noticed when he turned to face me his features had changed. His face had taken on a gray sheen and tusks had formed at the side of his mouth.

"I …… I don't know." I stuttered and pushed myself deeper into the couch. I remember the cops being called, the moving, and there's something else at the edge of my mind that's just not coming.

"I remember it well, Michael. I was starving Michael." He drew out the last few words to emphasize his statement. His tusks were growing longer, and his mouth had elongated, stretching itself into a trunk.

"This country is sick, Michael. Did you know that? Used to my kind, we would go around the nation helping people guarding people young and old alike. We were revered as GODS MICHAEL!"

He strode forward and shoved me deeper into the couch, tusks grazing my cheeks.

"Then your kind started getting sick, and we tried so hard to help you we tried to help all of you, but you starved us! You started taking pills that forced you to sleep. That took away your ability to dream, and I watched my brothers DIE MICHAEL!" He spat with rage, his body slowly changing from the calm doctor he had been. Now two huge bear's paws were bearing down on my shoulders.

"I thought we would die, Michael, then you came along. You and your failed suicide attempt brought you to me. They placed you on watch and I latched on. I waited so long for them to release you and even longer for you to stop taking the medicine."

He eased his weight off me and lumbered back towards his chair.

"I am a Baku Michael. I feed off your dreams and I keep evil far from you. Demons fear me, but don't worry. I can't harm you humans. I do, however, need to eat to exist. And while I can't harm you physically, I've been around for millennia. I will ensure your nightmares produce enough sustenance to sustain me and my brethren for as long as I can."

He glanced at the clock. No longer any semblance of the doctor remained, only a chimera of elephant and bear.

"I'm afraid we are out of time. Michael, let us begin our session."

I woke up drenched in sweat, my throat on fire, and a loud knocking coming from my front door. I opened it to see a shining badge and a very angry officer.

"Got a noise complaint from this apartment."

I tried to answer him, but all that came out was a whisper. He stared at me, and a half-grin broke out on his face, tusks showing from each corner of his mouth.

"Bad dreams again, Michael?"

Tap

Tap
Tap
Tap

"Look John, if you're that bored, you don't have to watch the movie," said Sara.

"I'm fine. I promise just little muscle twitches you know," I replied.

The movie started only 30 minutes ago. I had suggested it to keep her occupied for some time so I could deal with my thoughts. I really should have made a call, but I didn't want to move. I didn't want Sara getting concerned.

Tap
Tap
Tap

"Do you want to go take a breather outside?" asked Sara.

"I'm telling you I'm fine. Just trust me, please." I snapped.

"Okay, then grumpy." Sara huffed and locked herself into the tv again.

My phone sat in the kitchen and my concentration was stretched to the max. I had to figure out a way to get us out of this situation, and her constant questioning wasn't helping. I had to think I had to figure it out quickly.

Tap
Tap

"Seriously, John what the…"

Tap

"John, stop it now! You're ruining the movie!" Sara lost it.

"Sara…sweetheart…please for me, just let me do this, okay?" I pleaded.

"Why?"

Tap

Tap

Tap

"You know what? Don't even bother. I'm going to bed!" Sara stormed off.

I didn't even move my head. The last time I looked away from the window, it had moved about 50 yards. I could only make out the silhouette before that once I looked away and looked back, it had been standing not even ten feet from the window. It moved in between blinks until I could make out its pitch-black eyes after just a few minutes.

Its smile stretched as its gaze had met mine. Then he had lifted a bony finger. Sara had mistaken the taps for my boredom, but luckily, with her gone, I could focus on this thing without her noticing. A loud ring startled me, and I glanced at the kitchen where my phone was dancing along the countertop. I tore my gaze away and back to the window.

A frost etched smiley face was crudely drawn in the pane where the black-eyed man stood seconds ago.

Tap

Tap

Tap

"John, enough with the damn tapping! Hurry up and come to bed."

"Just a moment," I responded.

"Close the window, please. All the heat is getting out and I'm not getting back up."

The problem with Tony

Tony caught my eye one day as I made my rounds through the back alleys of this godforsaken town. He was humming along, passing the homeless, the downtrodden. The druggies never batted an eye at him. Tony was lost in his thoughts, head in the clouds, worldly problems were miles below him. I decided on a whim to follow him and see where his path led him and why he was so happy.

Tony's path led him down block after block of some of the seedier parts of town to a ramshackle little apartment complex. Tony entered the dingy foyer and entered the elevator with me in tow. Tony never acknowledged me, just kept right on humming away to that stupid happy little tune of his. I brushed up against him before the doors opened to see what his reaction might be, but he paid no mind and exited through the opened elevator doors.

Tony's apartment resembled the exterior almost to the T, with broken wallpaper, ripped carpet, and a moldy lingering smell. He went about his night in what must have been his routine shower, change, supper, tv, and finally bed. The next morning, he awoke and went off to work. He followed the same path home and followed the same routine. I had moved some things around in his apartment to gauge his reaction and, without skipping a beat, he would pick up the misplaced item and place it back right.

I spent a month trying to get a reaction out of Tony. When moving things wasn't enough, I moved on to moving things in front of him, which had zero effect. I tried all the typical paranormal rage-filled tricks. Slamming cabinets, appearing in dark mirrors, or right at the corner of your eye's sight line Tony was a steel wall of nonbelief, or so I thought.

One night, during a particularly rainy spell in the city, Tony didn't come home. I, an aggravated entity that I am, decided to wreck his apartment. How dare he break his routine and leave me here? The next day Tony came back and, like usual, took no heed to the disarray in his apartment. Tony meticulously set everything in its place and went about his nightly routine as if everything in his world was no different.

A month later, I grew bored with trying to get his attention at home and decided to meet him after work to try to liven things up. Tony left work at his usual prompt time, but instead of going left, he hailed a taxi. Tony sent the taxi on a complex tour of the city and after a 30-minute drive, the taxi deposited him on a corner near the warehouse district. Tony spent the next 30 minutes wandering down back alleys and side streets until darkness set.

After the streetlights came on, Tony wandered over to a row of warehouses and unlocked a set of heavy chains. Intrigued by this sudden change in routine. I clung to him, waiting to see what came next. Any other human would have shuddered and tried to brush me away, but Tony was a statue of indifference. We made our way down a flight of steps and Tony stood still for a few minutes next to an iron door set on the floor. His ears perked at a slight rustling until a bird flew away and all was quiet.

Tony shimmied down the iron ladder swiftly closing the door behind him. What awaited me at the bottom was a clean operating room. The amount of equipment in the room could rival any small clinic. A muffled scream from the corner caught my attention and when I saw where that scream came from, I learned a whole new appreciation for Tony. Sat in a steel chair bound and gagged was a middle-aged man in rags.

Tony wasted no time or words on this man. He quickly unbound him and forced him onto the table. He went about with surgical precision, slicing a tendon here and maiming a muscle there. Sewing the wound back up before he could bleed out, but doing nothing for the interior damage he had done. After operating on the man for close to 2 hours, Tony stood back and admired his handy work and, without a moment of hesitation, slit his carotid artery.

I floated there dumbstruck, and that's when I heard Tony say his first words.

"I grow very lonely, so a little company is nice to have, but I like things in their places."

He turned toward me and met my gaze for the first time.

"You were my first success, but I will not tolerate your childish antics any longer. The second one was a failure. He started screaming the minute he came back, but this time I think I got the kinks worked out."

Tony stared for a moment at the man bleeding out on the table before turning back to me.

"If not, there are always more companions out there for the taking. Now time for you to go. You've worn out your welcome with me. Exsurgat Deus et dissipentur inimici ejus: et fugiant qui oderunt eum a facie ejus. Sicut deficit fumus, deficiant: sicut fluit cera a facie ignis, sic pereant peccatores a......."

When the Cicadas Dance

"Mom, dad, I'm home!"

I made my way into their well-kept and spacious home and navigated my way into their all-purpose room, formerly known as the den. They were both dressed and ready for the day, basking in the sun that shone through the bay window. I noticed a note that had been attached to the back of dad's wheelchair written in Beth's scratchy scribble. "medicines all done tried breakfast. They didn't want any."

Beth had been their nurse for the better part of five years and had little to no difficulties dealing with the day-to-day life of caring for them. I decided to go and try to make them something to see if their appetite had come back. As I walked into the kitchen, I noticed something sitting on the window ledge outside. A cicada shell sat empty, facing into the house and in a flash, I was transported back to my youth and the terror of what those things are capable of. In the summer of 1986, my parents were the lead entomologists for the NISC (national invasive species council). They had been tasked with going to the Nantahala national forest at the southern edge of the Appalachian Mountains to inspect the insect population. With it being summer break, I was to accompany them and be their bag boy for the next month. With relative ease, dad had the camper loaded, a house sitter arranged, and the maps marked with the exact route we needed to go.

A mere 12 hours later, we arrived in Nantahala and discussed with the local rangers where we could set up and the best locations to visit for mom and dad to complete their research. Once we got our camper into place, I was left alone to explore while mom and dad set up their equipment and went over their maps. Nantahala was a beautiful mixture of old trees and winding creek beds, the perfect breeding grounds for any number of pests. After I had explored to my heart's content in the relatively small distance around our campsite, the smell of food brought me back to camp.

As I sat down at our table, a loud crunching sound made me jump. My mother dusted my backside off and showed me the remains of a cicada shell I had reduced to dust. "It's okay honey, this one's long gone. This is their mating time. You won't see these again for another 17 years." Mom said, dusting her hands off and going back to her food. I double-checked my seat and devoured my can of spaghetti. With no daylight left to us, we decided to call it a night and start at first light.

Most of our day was spent cataloging the typical species of grasshoppers, crickets, and mosquitoes. The rest of the day was spent hunting for the peskier insects. the one's mom and dad had been sent down here to find and determine how bad the issue was. Being from the city, it never occurred to me that the loud noises we were hearing were out of place until I had stepped on my tenth cicada shell. "The only invasive species are these cicadas it's almost like sitting at a demolition derby," Dad grumbled as he released yet another grasshopper back to the forest floor.

After dad had made it clear what the noise was, I couldn't help but fixate on it. Every time I would get near a cicada shell, I could feel the hum crescendo and then fade back as I got further away. I started counting just how many of the shells I saw on my walks with my parents.

"Dad, how many cicadas usually come out during their mating time?"

"a typical brood can be up to 400 if they all make it. Why do you ask?"

"I've counted almost 200 just today. Is that normal?" Dad shrugged me off and went back to his maps.

I dreamed of cicadas that night and woke up screaming about them. Their hum was so loud when I awoke that I could feel my skin vibrating. The next day I was so tired and shaken I kept myself in the camper and I hummed to myself to try and block the sound out. I used the restroom off the steps for fear of crunching on any more left-behind shells. My parents were concerned about me and told me we could leave in the morning. They hadn't found any invasive insects, and my health was a priority.

That night, the humming was so intense I could not sleep. I could hear it circling the camper, pulsating every few seconds, almost as if it was chanting. At midnight, I saw a shadow pass by the window above the sink and wings brush against the glass. My curiosity overcame my fear, and I grabbed the flashlight I kept under my pillow. The forest was bright with moonlight where it could split the tree canopy and utter blackness where the trees held dominion.

Every step I took into the woods was met with the crackle of a dead exoskeleton. The paths were lined with cicada shells, and I could see their previous hosts flying in the beams of moonlight. It was mesmerizing watching them dart in and out of the moonlight, losing sight of them in the dark only to reappear wings glistening a second later. I watched, awestruck, for what felt like hours, watching as the cicadas danced back and forth through the trees. I could hear a humming noise softer than the cicada's call and realized it was coming from my throat.

I was humming along with the cicadas in rhythm with their dance, swaying back and forth to their movements. A pair of eyes met mine from the shadow's red as a fresh wound and a humming chorus joined my own. The eyes bobbed and swayed to match my rhythm, and its humming intensified. I wanted to see this creature. I wanted to know what it was. I needed to know it. I started stepping toward the eyes, disregarding the crunch beneath my feet drawn into the humming that was matching my own. "Aron!"

My dad tackled me from behind and threw me back to my mom. My mother pushed me defensively behind herself while my dad stood at his tallest and held up his arms to make himself look bigger. Our connection had been broken and my mind had gone hazy. I couldn't remember walking into the woods or why my parents were here or why the two red eyes in the tree line were looking at us with such malice. My dad yelled at the creature, trying to scare it off, and with that last act of defiance, the hum of cicadas became too much, and I hit the ground, blood running from my ears.

I could no longer hear anything besides a tiny ringing sound in both ears, but my eyes worked well. A humanoid shape made entirely of matured cicadas emerged from the woods where the eyes had been and bore down on my dad. My mother enveloped me in a protective embrace, and darkness consumed me.

That was 17 years ago. With a cochlear implant, I can now hear the world around me again. My parents, on the other hand were left in a coma for several months and once they did awaken remained in a near vegetative state for the rest of the time. The NISC covered the medical bills and granted my parents' early retirement so they would be taken care of. I attended many therapy sessions throughout the years and can sleep better at night.

I tore my eyes away from the shell lying on the window ledge and made my way back into the den. I popped the lid off the yogurt I had brought for my parents and saw my dad's eye had a tear rolling down. I wiped it off and leaned into him. I could see his eyes making small figure eights while he stared out of the window and could hear a faint humming coming from his chest. I looked over at mom and noticed her eyes making the same pattern. Looking down at the windowsill, I noticed a line of cicadas swaying back and forth in time to mom and dad's eye movements. I could hear inside my head the humming that was coming from the woods, and I could feel the eyes on me even if I couldn't see them. 17 years ago, I watched the cicadas dance for the first time. As I felt my body begin to sway to their rhythm, I knew tonight I would get to see an encore.

A simple task

"It fucking lied to me! It told me that if I just did what it said, I could walk straight through those pearly bull shit gates, but guess what angels can lie just as well as devils."

So, let's not beat around the bush here. I know I'm not a saint or anything like that. I'm just a normal guy. I work a 9 to 5 and I stick to myself. I like it that way. It keeps me clean, and it keeps me sane. I am an inherently flawed human. I don't go to church or pray. I don't go out of my way to commit heinous acts of violence so you would think I would at least be considered for a spot in purgatory at least.

I read Dante's Divina Commedia. I know all about the different levels and what awaits me at those iconic locations. An eternity of wandering with no purpose lost to time and needs sounded perfect to me, better than going to one of the other 9 rings and suffering for all eternity. I can talk all day about my virtue or lack thereof, but I know I'm rambling, and I should just start putting the pieces together for you, my kind, observant listener.

I had spent my week in a funk stuck in the routine day-to-day menial office work sorting this file, shredding that one, taking this one to the boss, washing, rinsing, and repeating as necessary. Friday night, all I wanted to do was to sit on my ass in front of my tv and indulge in a little alcohol. My poison of choice being my best friend Jack and his buddy coke. I was a decent way into Wheel of Fortune and an even better way into the bottle when something went click and I don't mean a little tiny pop; I mean a whole damn CLICK.

The tv was too bright. The lights were damaging to the eyes and my walls were painted white. The entire room was sterile. I looked around, taking in my surroundings. It was my room alright, just different. Wheel of Fortune was still running through its routine, but my bottle was gone. A man in white approached me and started talking, but his words were cutting in and out.

"Is……. thing……… Johnson?"

I asked him where I was and where my damn bottle was. He stared at me for a minute and opened his mouth to say something when IT cut him off and dismissed him from the room. I almost pissed myself when I took in the full form of IT. This was no normal run-of-the-mill angel bathed in white light with the halo over its head. No, this was the mother of all angels' wings sprouting out of every nook and cranny of its big sideways eye with nobody in sight. When it spoke, its voice boomed in my mind.

"I know you are disoriented, but worry, not all will be well." IT boomed at me, and I winced away from it. Everything about it scared me with a deep instinctual fear. I wanted to run from this thing and a drop from a fifth-floor window was the last worry in my mind.

"Running will do no good, Mr. Johnson, and the window is locked."

"Why do you know that?" I replied.

The eye just regarded me with no response.

"I have a task for you. Can I entrust this task to you?"

"I don't think I can refuse you, honestly."

"You have free will, Mr. Johnson. It's just a simple task, so will you refuse or accept?"

"What do I get from this?" I asked sheepishly. "I can guarantee a nice worry-free stay here."

"So where is here exactly?"

"Where do you think here is?

White walls, white furniture, white clothes. This is heaven. It must be. It is perfect and sterile, so it must be.

"Heaven?" I suggested.

The eye boomed laughter as I tried to hold my ears to protect against the sound.

"All I need you to do is drink this water." He glanced at the cup on the end table beside the chair that I hadn't seen before. I downed it without hesitation. If this was all it took to secure a spot in heaven, then I couldn't refuse.

"Thank you, Mr. Johnson get some rest I will be seeing you again shortly."

The lights dimmed to a comfortable glow and the sounds of Wheel of Fortune came flooding back in. My dingy apartment with its tan walls and green carpet showed no sign of the sterile whiteness they had shown shortly before. The bottle of Jack laid empty next to me. "I'm going to regret this tomorrow." I thought as my eyelids became heavy.

I awoke to a normal sunny day, birds singing, cars honking outside, and no hangover. I spent my day running through normal errands. While out grocery shopping, I saw a reflection of the angel in one of the cooler doors and screamed. Everyone around me stared and backed away. They would have a reason to scream if they could see him, too. A crackle of static burst through the speakers, followed by "a simple task, Mr. Johnson." The lights surged and every tiny noise was a boom in my head. I dropped my crap and ran out of there.

I ran back to my apartment and opened a bottle of my old friend. We didn't invite his other buddy. This was just mine and his time. I turned on the tv trying to find something to distract me from what I had heard and saw there was nothing but static. The lights in my apartment surged and popped all at once. Casting darkness throughout my apartment regardless of the bright sunny day that had just been filtering in through the window.

"A simple task, Mr. Johnson, then you can. "

IT's voice was swimming in and out. His words were coming out loud, then to a whisper, bouncing back and forth with every syllable.

"What do you want from me now?" I screamed.

"Relax, Mr. Johnson, all I want from you is to drink this glass of water."

I downed it again and asked *it* just how long I needed to do this for.

"As long as it takes, Mr. Johnson."

"You made a promise!" I screamed at *it*.

"And I will keep my promise, Mr. Johnson. I'm just waiting for a spot to open."

"How the fuck do spots open in heaven?" I yelled and launched myself out of my chair. I knew it was foolish to try to fight *it*, but my sanity wasn't quite there. In an instant *it* had moved back to the far wall, and I landed face first on my green-carpeted floor. The tv static and puddle of Jack under me woke me up several hours later. I went to my bed and tossed and turned until sunlight chased the darkness away.

I stayed inside the next day curled up into myself on the chair, tv blaring. Every hour, the screen would go static while "a simple task" would blare through the speakers. I turned off the lights, afraid they would blow again. I drank glass after glass of whiskey, hoping to force myself to sleep to make it all stop and go away. Around 7 at night, my entire apartment shook and turned into the white sterile room I dreaded. *It* appeared before me again the glee in its eye at my appearance was noticeable without facial features.

"No more, please. If this is how you get into heaven, I don't want it. You can throw me into the deepest pit right next to Satan for all I care!" I yelled at *it* and swung my pillow to keep *it* at bay.

"Last time Mr. Johnson and I will leave you be, just drink the water."

"Swear to me, this is the last time!" I roared at *it*.

"You have no reason to doubt me."

I drank the water.

It faded out while my apartment faded back into view, and I finally slept.

The next day I went to work. I washed, rinsed, and repeated my usual work schedule and I went home to my nonsterile apartment then I went to sleep.

 The next day I went to work. I washed, rinsed, and repeated my usual work schedule and I went home to my nonsterile apartment, then I went to sleep.

The next day, I went to work. I washed, rinsed, and repeated my usual work schedule and I went home to my nonsterile apartment, then I went to sleep.

The next day, I went to work. I washed, rinsed, and repeated my usual work schedule and I went home to my nonsterile apartment, then I went to sleep.

"Time of death 7:05 pm October 3rd, 2026, patient Kevin Johnson pronounced dead from alcohol poisoning by Dr. Jim Woodall."

Dr. Woodall clicked off his recorder and glared at the nurse.

"It was a simple task, but even that is too hard for you."

A trip to lock head woods

A trip to lock head woods was all my parents talked about for months before the summer break started. My dad told wondrous tales of his childhood adventures to my brother and me every chance he got. While my mother told us all about the wonderful Girl Scout trips she took. It sounded ever so magical to a teenager who would spend most of the time babysitting his little brother, who had the survival instincts of a lemming.

Months came and went, and the school bell rang for the last time for some. On a warm July morning, dad loaded us into his failing Tahoe,
Bound for Lock Head woods. Urban claustrophobia gave way to the rural sparseness of the great national forest, and a few hours later, lock head woods came into view.

We spent an hour unpacking and setting up the campsite. For all my uncertainties, it was nice to be out of the city and breathing in the fresh air. Dad led us on a nature hike that was more of a can you guess what bug is biting you and how badly it will hurt later tour that squashed my upbeat disposition fairly quickly. Our "hike" ended at a beautiful rock outcropping that looked over an impossibly blue pond surrounded by tall pines. Dad promised to take us there the following day to swim if the weather cooperated.

The sun was going down as we made our way back to the campsite and we all set about getting a fire set up. We ate our hot dogs and chips by the light of the fire while dad regaled us with all the classic ghost stories. The machete-wielding killer hiding in the woods, the ghost that only comes out during a full moon in these exact woods, and of course, the shapeshifter that mimics your loved ones. After the food and stories, we cleaned up and packed ourselves up for a good night's rest, my parents in one tent and me and my brother in the other.

A rustling sound from outside the tent stirred me from a fitful sleep. My brother going to the bathroom I assumed until a loud snore next to me caused me to sit upright. I opened the tent just a crack to check and see what the sound was. My dad was standing next to the fire pit, eyes blank. "dad." I called to him to make sure he was okay as soon as he heard me call out to him. His head snapped towards me.

His eyes were milky white, and blood was pouring from his nose. I screamed and backed away from the entrance, trying to put as much distance between myself and him as I could. The scream woke my brother up and before he could even utter a syllable; I had my hand clamped down on his mouth. He took the hint and kept quiet. I strained my ears to hear any sounds outside, but it was dead silent. No insects or animals dared call out. I was ready to peek out again to see if maybe I was just imagining the whole thing when the light from the opening was blocked, and that milky white eye peered in on us both.

"Boys..."

His eyes lit up, and a smile stretched his face into an unpleasant clown mask ringed with blood from his pouring nose.

"Boys, boys, boys, won't you join me? I have some marvelous stories to tell you! I told them to your mother already and she just about died of excitement."

His voice had taken a higher pitch than normal and the way he enunciated died unnerved me. This was my dad's body, but it wasn't my dad.

"Well, if you won't come to me, I guess I'll JUST COME TO YOU!"

I screamed as hard as I could and kicked blindly out at him, but his target wasn't me. It was my brother, who sat stupefied. Dad yanked him up and in a flash bit into his throat. I watched the light fade out of his eyes and his head sag. Dad's hands fell on my shoulders and as I felt the teeth tear through the flesh of my throat, I felt something else.

I was shaken awake by my dad, his face inches away from my own.

"Jesus kid, you were screaming bloody murder, no more scary stories for you before bed."

I surveyed the campsite and saw my mom and brother sitting by the small fire eating breakfast. I shakingly got up and sat with them while dad gave me a plate.

"Are you going to be okay?"

"Yeah, dad I'm fine just a bad dream."

That day was just about as magical as you can get after seeing your dad turn into a psychopath in a dream where you felt his teeth rip out your own throat. We swam in the pond, fished when we were too tired from swimming, and ate the fish we caught for lunch. Dad took us on another nature walk this time. Thankfully, the bug spray was effective, and we could enjoy ourselves.

Dad skipped the stories that night, worried it might cause another nightmare. The hot dogs were hot, and the s'mores were the perfect amount of coma-inducing sugar overload you would need right before bed. I dreaded sleep, but it enveloped me as soon as my eyes closed.

I woke up to another rustling sound, this time in the tent with me instead.

"You're awake! You're awake! You're awake!"

I spun around to the high-pitched childish voice and came face to face with my younger brother. His milk-white eyes stared into mine while a clown mask smile spread across his face. I screamed in shock and backpedaled towards the entrance of the tent.

"I've been waiting for you, brother! You're going to miss all the fun!!!"

An icy hand gripped my shoulder from behind and pulled me out of the tent. My dad was standing there grinning at me in the light of the moon. "You must join us, son. I have so many stories to tell you."

I tried to kick and squirm, but his grip on me was too strong. My brother came out of the tent in a rictus walk and lurched his way towards us.

"Dad told me his stories and I know you will love them; brother, please join us."

His mouth stretched so wide I heard his jaw pop, and he sank his teeth into my wrist before I could react. Pain flared throughout my body as he pulled away veins and muscle tissue. My nerve endings screamed as they were exposed to the air for the first time. I screamed for my mother and her soft voice carried from the tent she shared with dad.

"You should listen to your father, dear. Join us and listen."

Two white eyes shone through the tent flap, and I slipped away, no longer able to bear the pain. I woke up slowly, my body screaming at me with every movement. My head felt like splitting. I couldn't focus my eyes due to the pain.

"We have a live one! I see movement in the back."

My eyes slowly focused in, but I couldn't move my head. The pain was too much, and I felt unconsciousness trying to take over again. Two white eyes were staring at me in the seat next to me, dried blood caked around the gaping wound on my brother's forehead.

"Don't move! We are coming to get you!"

I couldn't move even if I wanted. My eyes were locked on my brother's face. I moved my eyes slightly and saw my mom and dad's milky eyes staring up from the reflection of the rearview. My throbbing head finally came to terms with what was happening, and I screamed.

"It's okay! We are getting you out. Just stay calm!"

I screamed as hard as my dry throat would let me until I felt the cold calmness of unconsciousness creeping over me. Before I could pass out completely, I heard a collective whisper.

"Join us"

I awoke two days later; besides a few bruised ribs and dehydration, the only damage was in my head. My whole family had passed away in the accident. The doctors tried to give it to me easily, but I knew it before I had passed out. I went to live with some relatives out of state after the funeral and I've been seeing a psychiatrist to help me cope with the loss, but I can't be honest with them.

My family visits me every night just as I'm fading into sleep, their eyes always drilling into my own, telling me to join them. I refuse them time after time, but I just can't keep this up. I know why they want me to. It's not because of some crappy survivor's guilt if I had just told dad about the puddle of brake fluid under the truck that morning they would still be here. When they come tonight, I'm going to ask dad to tell me a story. I hope it's a good one. The pills I took are making it hard to stay awake.

The end.

Or it's not, who knows. You made it to the other side of the path. That is a tremendous feat. You should be patting yourself on the back. With your own arm, though, not the one you found along the way.

Heed my words, friend.

This was but a small part of the journey.
Madness lies ahead. Prepare yourself.

Yours truly

Z. Martin